Tommy Visits the Doctor

By
Jean H. Seligmann
and
Milton I. Levine, M.D.

Illustrated by Richard Scarry

A GOLDEN BOOK • NEW YORK
Western Publishing Company, Inc.
Racine, Wisconsin 53404

The publishers hope that this little book will help prepare a child for his visit to the doctor. It was written by two people who have worked extensively with children, and it was illustrated by Richard Scarry, who believes that rabbits go to doctors, too.

Today Tommy is going to visit Doctor Brown.
Doctor Brown is not a doctor for mommies.
He is not a doctor for daddies.
Doctor Brown is a doctor for children.
Doctor Brown is Tommy's doctor.

And Bobby Bunny is going to visit Doctor Smiles.
Doctor Smiles is a doctor for bunnies.

Tommy is not sick.

Tommy wants to show Doctor Brown how big he is growing. He wants Doctor Brown to see how strong he is.

And Bobby wants Doctor Smiles to see how well he is.

Tommy rings the door bell at the doctor's office. Doctor Brown's nurse opens the door and smiles at Tommy.

"Come in, Tommy," she says. "Doctor Brown will be ready to see you in a few minutes."

Bobby's doctor has a nice nurse, too.

Tommy sees his friend Sally in the waiting room. She has just been to see the doctor.

"Hi, Tommy," says Sally. "I have grown two inches since last time."

"That's great!" says Tommy.

Bobby's friend Fluffy says, "I'm one whole pound heavier!"

Tommy rides on the rocking horse.

*And Bobby plays
with a red truck.*

Soon Doctor Brown comes out and says, "Hello, Tommy, come in. It's your turn now."

They go into Doctor Brown's office.

"Now Tommy," says Doctor Brown, "the first thing you do is take off your shoes and socks and shirt and slacks."

Bobby takes off his clothes, too.

"Now, let's get up on the scale and see how heavy you are."

Doctor Brown looks at the scale and says, "You weigh forty pounds. That's five pounds more than the last time you were here! Your mommy must be feeding you well."

"My," says Doctor Smiles, "what a fine big rabbit you are!"

"I eat all my carrots," says Bobby proudly.

"Did you grow taller, too?" asks Doctor Brown.

"Yes," says Tommy. "Last year's coat is too short."

"Let's see how much you grew," says Doctor Brown. "Stand as tall as you can."

Doctor Brown measures Tommy.

"Indeed you did grow! Last time you were just this tall," says Doctor Brown. "You grew this much."

Doctor Brown holds his hands to show Tommy how much he grew.

Bobby Bunny has grown, too. "Especially your ears," says Doctor Smiles.

"Now hop on this table," says Doctor Brown. "I'm going to look into your ears." He takes out something that looks like a flashlight with a tiny light at the end of it.

"First let's look in this ear. Now the other.

"Good," says Doctor Brown. "You've got two fine ears."

Bobby's ears are much bigger than Tommy's.

That's because Bobby has rabbit ears.

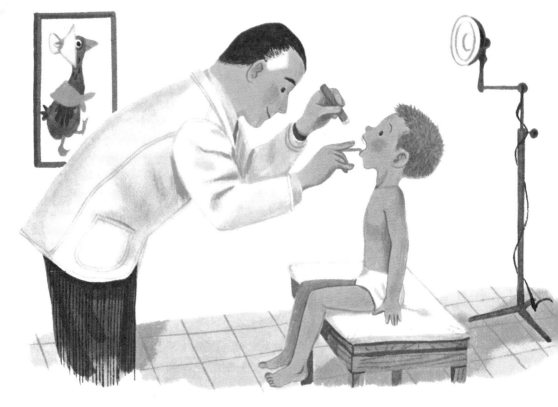

"And now," says Doctor Brown, "I'm going to look into your mouth and count your teeth. 1, 2, 3, 4, 5, 6, 7, 8, 9, 10 on the top, and 1, 2, 3, 4, 5, 6, 7, 8, 9, 10 on the bottom. That's twenty teeth, and just right for your age. Be sure you take good care of them."

Bobby has just enough teeth for a healthy little rabbit.

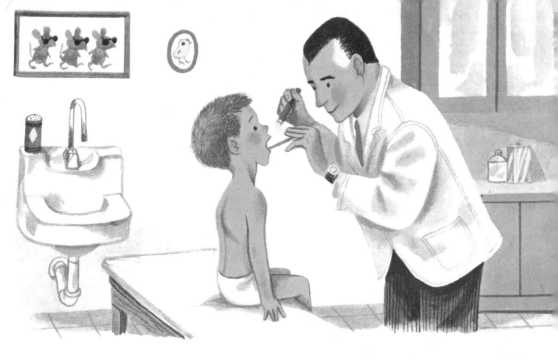

"Next," says Doctor Brown, "I want to look way down your throat. Can you open your mouth very, very wide? That's fine. And now, while your mouth is open, stick out your tongue and say 'a-a-a-ah.' That's very good. Your throat looks fine."

Doctor Smiles looks down Bobby's throat, too.

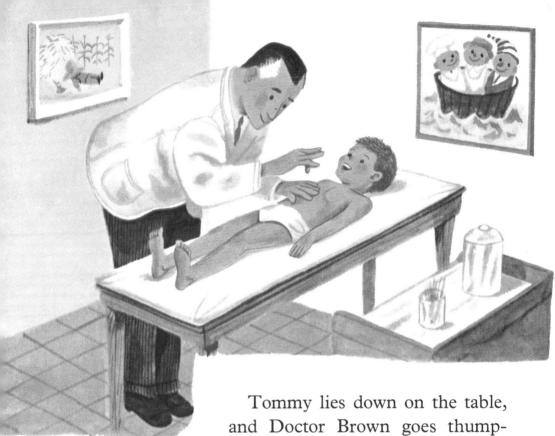

Tommy lies down on the table, and Doctor Brown goes thump-thump-thump all over Tommy's chest.

He does the same thing on Tommy's back. It sounds like a little drum.

Bobby laughs when Doctor Smiles goes thump-thump. He is a tickly rabbit.

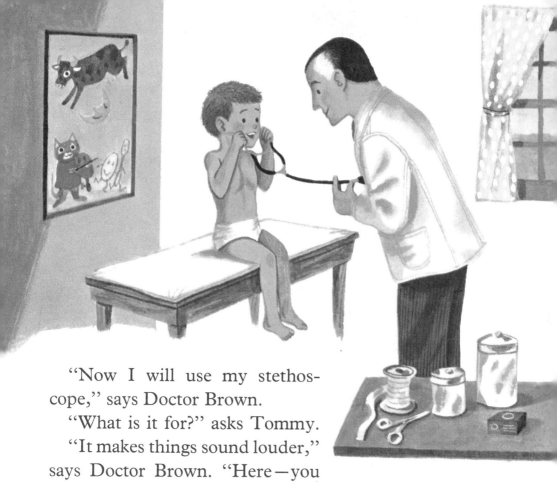

"Now I will use my stethoscope," says Doctor Brown.

"What is it for?" asks Tommy.

"It makes things sound louder," says Doctor Brown. "Here—you can listen to my heart with it."

Tommy hears Doctor Brown's heart going boom-boom-boom-boom.

And Bobby hears Doctor Smiles' heart go bumpity-bumpity-bump!

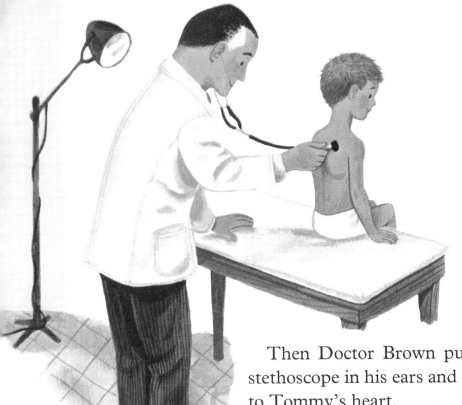

Then Doctor Brown puts the stethoscope in his ears and listens to Tommy's heart.

He listens to other sounds all over Tommy's chest and back.

"You sound just fine, young man," he tells Tommy.

"You sound just fine, young rabbit," says Doctor Smiles.

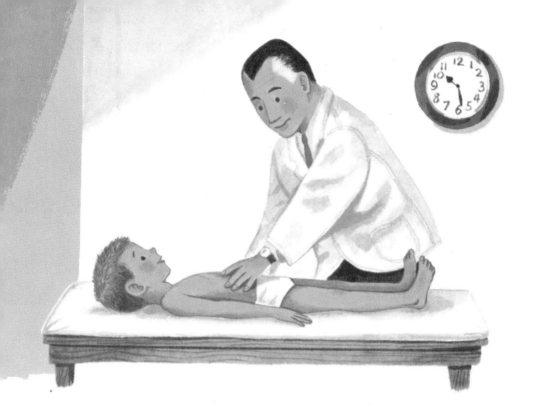

Tommy lies down again, and Doctor Brown feels his stomach.

Tommy is very ticklish. He can't help giggling.

*Bobby giggles too,
and wiggles his ears.*

"Now sit up, Tommy, and dangle your legs over the table."

The doctor holds up a little rubber hammer.

"If I hit the right spot on the knee," says Doctor Brown, "your foot jumps up all by itself. Watch."

He taps Tommy's knee very lightly with the hammer, and Tommy's foot jumps up.

"Look, my foot jumps up by itself," says Bobby. *"Do it again!"*

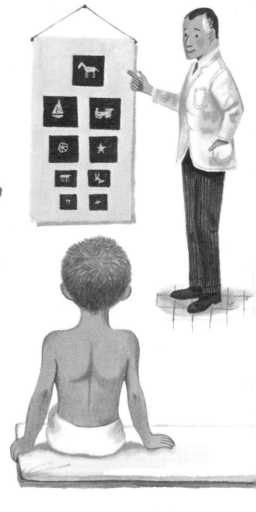

"Now," says Doctor Brown, "How well can you see? I'll show you some pictures."

Tommy looks. "That one is a horse!" he says.

The doctor points to another picture.

"That's a star!" says Tommy.

He looks at more pictures, and he knows what every one of them is.

"Good!" says Doctor Brown. "You see very well."

Doctor Smiles shows Bobby pictures, too.

Doctor Brown looks at a card that has Tommy's name at the top.

"I see you need a shot this time, Tommy."

"What is a shot like?" asks Tommy.

"It feels like a quick pin prick, and it's over in a second," says Doctor Brown. "This shot will keep you well and strong."

Bobby needs a shot, too.

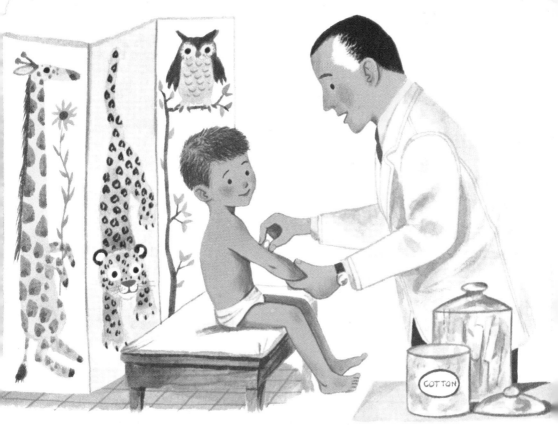

Tommy holds out his arm. The doctor rubs Tommy's skin with a piece of cotton wet with alcohol.

"That's to make sure your skin is clean," says the doctor. "By the time you take a deep breath, the shot will be over."

And it is!

"That wasn't so bad," says Bobby.

Just then the nurse comes in. She has some lollipops in her hand. "Choose one!" she tells Tommy.

"Thank you," says Tommy. "I'll take a red one!"

Bobby's nurse gives him a yellow balloon.

"All right, Tommy, you can get dressed now," says Doctor Brown. "You are a very healthy boy. When you come again we'll see how much more you have grown."
Tommy and his mother say good-bye to the doctor.

Bobby gets dressed.
"Good-bye, Doctor Smiles," says Bobby.

Tommy can hardly wait to get home.
He wants to tell his daddy how much he has grown.
"How pleased Daddy will be!" says Mommy.

"What a fine healthy bunny I have,"
says Mr. Rabbit.